JE MOZELLE
Mozelle, Shirley.
Zack's alligator

Dear Parent:
Your child's love of reading starts here!

Every child learns to read in a different way and at his or her own speed. Some go back and forth between reading levels and read favorite books again and again. Others read through each level in order. You can help your young reader improve and become more confident by encouraging his or her own interests and abilities. From books your child reads with you to the first books he or she reads alone, there are I Can Read Books for every stage of reading:

SHARED READING
Basic language, word repetition, and whimsical illustrations, ideal for sharing with your emergent reader

BEGINNING READING
Short sentences, familiar words, and simple concepts for children eager to read on their own

READING WITH HELP
Engaging stories, longer sentences, and language play for developing readers

READING ALONE
Complex plots, challenging vocabulary, and high-interest topics for the independent reader

ADVANCED READING
Short paragraphs, chapters, and exciting themes for the perfect bridge to chapter books

I Can Read Books have introduced children to the joy of reading since 1957. Featuring award-winning authors and illustrators and a fabulous cast of beloved characters, I Can Read Books set the standard for beginning readers.

A lifetime of discovery begins with the magical words "I Can Read!"

Visit www.icanread.com for information
on enriching your child's reading experience.

For Sally, Nancy, Nina—
and Uncle Alfred

HarperCollins®, 🐊®, and I Can Read Book® are trademarks of HarperCollins Publishers.

Zack's Alligator Text copyright © 1989 by Shirley Mozelle Illustrations copyright © 1989 by James Watts All rights reserved. No part of this book may be used or reproduced in any manner whatsoever without written permission except in the case of brief quotations embodied in critical articles and reviews. Manufactured in China. For information address HarperCollins Children's Books, a division of HarperCollins Publishers, 10 East 53rd Street, New York, NY 10022. www.harpercollinschildrens.com

Library of Congress Cataloging-in-Publication Data
Mozelle, Shirley.
  Zack's alligator / by Shirley Mozelle ; illustrated by James Watts.
    p.   cm.—(An I can read book)
  Summary: When Zack soaks his new alligator keychain in water, it grows into a full-sized and fun-loving alligator.
  ISBN-10: 0-06-444186-5 (pbk.) — ISBN-13: 978-0-06-444186-5 (pbk.)
  [1. Alligators—Fiction.] I. Watts, James, 1955– , ill. II. Title. III. Series.
PZ7.M868Zac 1989
[E]
                                                                                        88-32069
                                                                                        CIP
                                                                                        AC

I Can Read!

READING 2 WITH HELP

Zack's Alligator

story by **Shirley Mozelle**

pictures by **James Watts**

■ HarperCollins*Publishers*

A big box came in the mail for Zack.

It was from Zack's uncle Jim

in Florida.

Zack shook the box.

What could it be? he wondered.

He untied the bow

and ripped off the paper.

There was another box inside.

Zack lifted the lid.

Inside was an alligator key chain,
with a note from Uncle Jim.
It said,

Zack held up the key chain.

"This must be Bridget," he said.

Zack put Bridget in the sink
and turned on the faucet.

Bridget began to move—
her head turned,
her tail curled.

Bridget grew bigger

and bigger.

Soon she filled the sink.

Zack moved Bridget to the tub
and turned on the shower.
Bridget stretched and sighed.
"That feels *so* good!" she said.
Zack watched.

Bridget grew larger
and larger.
She grew out of the tub
and over the side.

Bridget moaned and groaned
and whipped her tail.
She splashed water everywhere.
"What is going on in there?"
called Zack's mother.
"I am watering the alligator,"
said Zack.
"Alligator! What alligator?"
"The one Uncle Jim sent," Zack said.
He heard his mother laugh.
"I see," she said.
"Well, clean up when you are done."
"I will," said Zack.

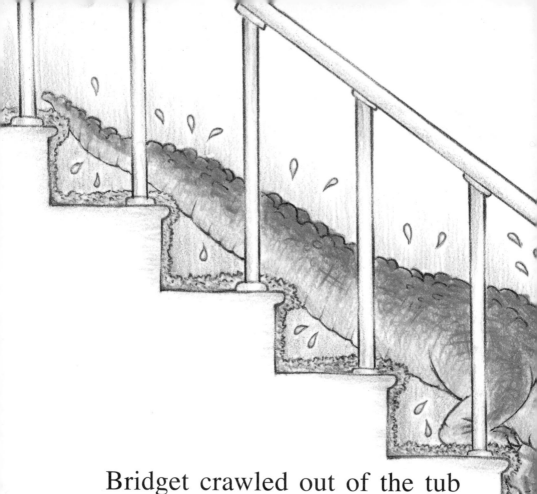

Bridget crawled out of the tub
and onto the floor.

"I am hungry," she said.

"Do you have any fish?"

"I don't know," said Zack.

"Let's go see."

Bridget followed Zack
down the stairs
and into the kitchen.

Zack opened the refrigerator door.

"No fish?" said Bridget.

"No," said Zack. "No fish.

But here is some meat loaf.

I can fix you a Meat Loaf Special!"

"What is that?" asked Bridget.

"A surprise," said Zack.

"I love surprises!" said Bridget.

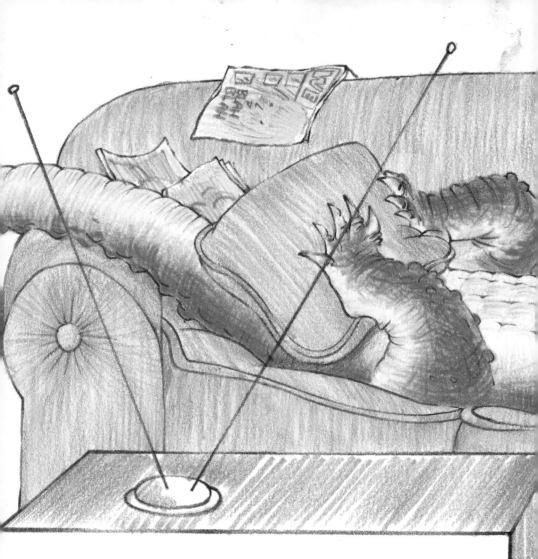

Bridget went into the living room
and stretched out on the sofa.

The sofa shook.

Bridget looked at the TV.

"What a funny-looking box!"

she said.

Then she hollered to Zack,

"Hurry up with the food!"

"I am coming!" said Zack.

21

He was making

his Meat Loaf Special—

meat loaf, peanut butter,

mustard, banana,

and a couple of pickles.

"Zack, what are you doing?"

asked his mother.

"I am fixing some meat loaf

for Bridget."

"Who is Bridget?"

"The alligator," said Zack.

"Oh, of course," said Mother.

"Well, save some for dinner."

"I will," said Zack.

Bridget ate every bite

of Zack's Meat Loaf Special.

"Delicious!" she said.

"I have never eaten anything

like that before.

Back home in the Glades,

I eat mostly fish

and snakes and slugs."

Suddenly Bridget jumped up
from the sofa.

"Time for a walk," she said.

Bridget wobbled to the door.

Zack followed.

Bridget's long tail

knocked over a chair

and some books off a table.

Zack picked up the chair
and the books.

"We are going out, Mom," he called.

"We?" she asked.

"Oh, yes, you and Bridget.

I forgot.

Well, don't be too long.

Dad will be home soon."

Outside, Bridget was wrestling
with the garden hose.
"I will get you," she growled.
She gave the hose a big bite.
Water squirted everywhere.

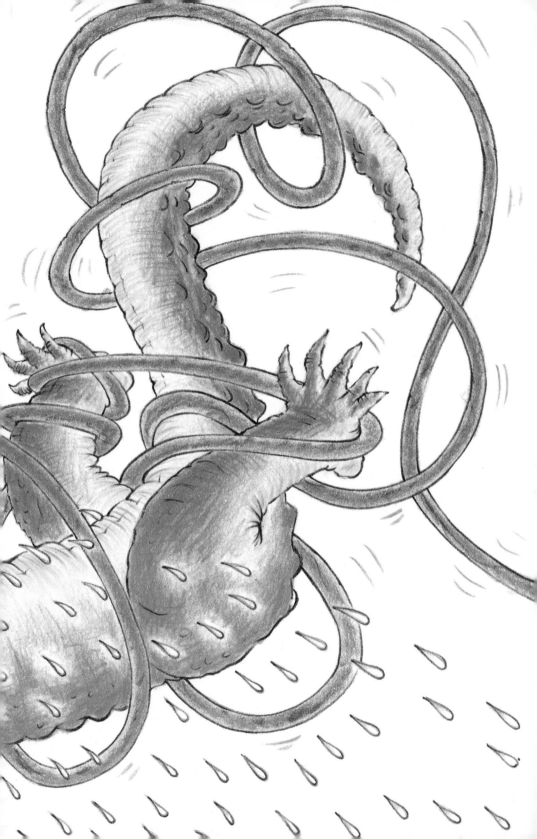

Zack ran to turn off the water.

"That snake will not bother anyone

ever again!" said Bridget.

Zack sighed and shook his head.

Bridget took off down the sidewalk.

Zack followed.

Just then the mailman

pulled up in his truck.

"What is that?" cried Bridget.

Before Zack could answer,

Bridget attacked!

She bit the tire of the truck.

Air hissed out.

35

"Dogs are bad enough,"

shouted the mailman,

"but I cannot handle this.

No, sir! Not alligators!"

The mailman jumped into his truck

and drove away with a flat tire.

Klump! Klump! Klump!

Bridget shook her head.

"I am glad we don't have those

in the Glades," she said.

Zack tried to say something,

but Bridget was off again.

They came to the park.

Bridget wanted to swing.

After that,

she climbed the monkey bars.

Then she jumped on the seesaw.

Zack had never seen anyone

seesaw by herself.

Next, Bridget ran

to the merry-go-round.

Round and round she went.

Bridget began to sing.

"Oh, I am a gator from the Glades,

and I can do anything—

and I mean anything!"

Bridget got so dizzy,

she fell off the merry-go-round.

Zack helped Bridget up.

Just then his best friend, Turk,

rode up on his bicycle.

"Hey, Zack!" said Turk.

"Where did you get that alligator?"

"From my uncle Jim," said Zack.

"Some uncle!" Turk said.

Suddenly Bridget shouted,

"What's that fuzzy-wuzzy?"

The woman took one look at Bridget
and picked up her dog.

"Come on, Poopsie," she said.

"Let Mama take you home."

Bridget did a cartwheel.

"Who would want

that fuzzy-wuzzy anyway?" she said.

"I am thirsty, not hungry."

Bridget did a quick one-two,

and hop-skipped to the fountain.

She drank big gulps of water.

Zack and Turk watched.

"Will you bring Bridget to school?"

asked Turk.

"I don't know," said Zack.

A policeman came over.

"You need a leash

for that alligator," he said.

"There is a law, you know!"

"Yes, sir," said Zack.

The policeman frowned.

"Well, keep him under control."

"*Him?*" cried Bridget.

"Well, I beg his pardon!

How rude!

Hasn't he ever seen

a girl gator before?"

"You should bring her to school,"
said Turk.

"Maybe," said Zack.

Zack and Turk rode Bridget
around the park.

Suddenly Bridget started to shrink.

"I need more water," she said.

Zack and Turk helped her

to the fountain.

Bridget slurped the cool water.

"This place is too dry," she said.

"In the Glades,

there is plenty of water

and moss and tall grass."

"What are the Glades?" asked Turk.

"The Everglades," said Zack.

"They are in Florida,

where my uncle Jim lives."

"Do you think

he could send me an alligator?"

asked Turk.

"I don't know," said Zack.

"I will ask him."

"That would be great!" said Turk.

"We have to go now," said Zack.

"Don't forget to bring Bridget
to school!" yelled Turk.

"Oh, please!" Bridget said to Zack.

"I want to see what school is like!"

"We will see," said Zack.

On the way home,

Bridget was shrinking more and more.

She looked up at Zack

with big, shiny alligator eyes.

"Will you water me again?" she asked.

"I will water you every day,"

said Zack.

"Good!" said Bridget.

Bridget was getting smaller
and smaller.

She bobbed her head up and down
and began singing.

"I am a gator from the Glades,

and I like to have fun every day.

Oh, yeah!"

When they got home,

Bridget was key chain size.

Zack put her safely in his pocket.

"Hello," said Zack's father.

"Your mother said

you were out with the alligator.

May I see it?"

"Yes, sir," said Zack.

Zack pulled out the key chain

with a small alligator

hanging from it.

"That's very nice," said his father.

"Now go wash up for dinner."

Zack went upstairs to his room.

He could hear

his mother tell his father

they would have chicken for dinner

instead of meat loaf.

"Are you all right?" whispered Zack.

"Never better," Bridget said.

She yawned.

"Don't forget to water me tomorrow."

"I won't," said Zack.

Zack put Bridget back in his pocket.

"Zack!" called Mother.

"Dinner is ready."

"I am coming!" Zack called back.

Zack felt Bridget move.

He patted his pocket
and smiled.

63